THE LITTLE OLD WOMAN
WHO USED HER HEAD
AND OTHER STORIES

She used her head and she used her head.

THE LITTLE OLD WOMAN
WHO USED HER HEAD
AND OTHER STORIES

by

Hope Newell

PICTURES BY

MARGARET RUSE

AND *C.1*

ANN MERRIMAN PECK

THOMAS NELSON INC.
NASHVILLE / NEW YORK

Second printing

Library of Congress Cataloging in Publication Data
Newell, Hope (Hockenberry)
The little old woman who used her head and other stories.

SUMMARY: Nineteen adventures of the little old woman who had such problems to solve as keeping her geese warm during the winter while taking their feathers for a feather bed.
[1. Humorous stories] I. Ruse, Margaret, illus.
II. Peck, Anne Merriman, 1884–   illus.
III. Title.
PZ7.N479Li5   [E]   73–17036
ISBN 0–8407–6328–X

CONTENTS

TO MY SON

JIMMIE

THE LITTLE OLD WOMAN
WHO USED HER HEAD
AND OTHER STORIES

1. The Little Old Woman

ONCE upon a time there was a Little Old Woman. She lived in a little yellow house with a blue door and two blue window boxes. In each of the window boxes there were yellow tulips.

All around her house was a neat blue fence. Inside the fence was the Little Old Woman's soup garden. She called it a soup garden because she raised vegetables in it, to cook in her soup. She raised carrots, potatoes, turnips, garlic, cabbages and onions.

The Little Old Woman was very poor. If she had not been so clever, she probably could not have made both ends meet. But she was a great one for using her head. She always said, "What is the good of having a head if you don't use it?"

So, as you will see, she managed to get along very well.

2. How She Got a Feather Bed

THE Little Old Woman had only one blanket for her bed. It was a nice red flannel blanket, but it was full of holes.

"I must get a new blanket before winter comes," she said. "Or better yet, I might buy me a feather bed. How warm and cozy I would be in a feather bed on cold winter nights!"

But feather beds cost a lot of money, so the Little Old Woman bought a flock of geese instead. As she was driving them home from the market, she said to herself:

"These twelve geese will lay eggs for me all summer. Then when winter comes I will pluck their feathers and make myself a feather bed. What a clever Old Woman I am!"

When the Little Old Woman arrived home, she drove the geese into the yard and closed the gate. Then she ate her supper and went to bed.

The next morning she heard a great noise in the yard.

When she opened the door the geese came running to her.

"Honk, honk!" said the big gander, flapping his wings.

"Honk, honk!" said all the other geese, flapping their wings.

Everywhere she went, the twelve geese followed her, saying, "Honk, honk!" and flapping their wings.

"Dear me," said the Little Old Woman, "I do believe they want something to eat. I must buy them some corn."

So she went to the market and bought a bag of corn for the geese.

Every morning when she opened the door, the geese came running to her.

"Honk, honk!" they said, flapping their wings.

Then she remembered to give them some corn.

The geese ate so much corn that pretty soon the Little Old Woman had to buy another bag of corn. After a while, that bag was empty too, and she had to buy another bag of corn.

"These geese eat a lot of corn," she said, "but after all, they are growing bigger and bigger. Their feathers are growing thicker and thicker. They will make me a fine feather bed when winter comes."

By and by the nights began to grow cold. The red flannel blanket was so full of holes that it did not keep the Little Old Woman warm. She shivered all night long.

"Winter will soon be here," she thought. "It is high time I plucked the geese and made my feather bed."

The next morning she went out to pluck the geese.

"How warm and contented they look," said the Little Old Woman. "They will be cold if I pluck their feathers. Maybe if I cut the holes out of the red blanket, it will be warm enough for me."

But when she fetched her scissors and cut the holes out of the red blanket, the holes were still there. In fact, they were bigger than ever.

"What am I to do?" she thought. "If I take their

feathers, the geese will be cold. If I do not take their feathers, I will be cold. I suppose I had better use my head."

And here is how the Little Old Woman used her head. First she tied a wet towel around her forehead. Then she sat down with her forefinger against her nose and shut her eyes.

She used her head and used her head and used her head. She used her head so long that it began to ache, but finally she knew what to do.

"The red blanket is no good to me," she said. "I will cut it into twelve pieces and make each of the geese a warm red coat. Then I can pluck their feathers to make me a feather bed."

The Little Old Woman set to work and made each of the geese a little red coat. On each coat she sewed three shiny brass buttons.

"Now I must pluck the geese and make my feather bed," said the Little Old Woman.

She took a basket and went out to pluck the geese. She plucked the big gander and put his feathers in the basket. She plucked the gray goose and put her feathers into the basket. Then she plucked the other geese and put their feathers into the basket.

When all the geese were plucked, the Little Old Woman put a little red coat on each goose and fastened it with the shiny brass buttons.

"How handsome the geese look," she said. "I was very clever to think of making the little red coats to keep them warm."

Then she carried the basket of feathers into the house and sewed them into a strong ticking to make a feather bed.

When the bed was all finished, the Little Old Woman said to herself:

"I shall sleep very warm this winter. How wise I was to buy a flock of geese to make a feather bed. It all comes of using my head."

3. How She Saved Her Corn

THE Little Old Woman was bothered with rats. They gnawed holes in the bag of corn that she kept for the geese, and carried away the corn. They got in the cupboard and ate her victuals. They made nests in her bureau drawers. There were eight of them in all.

"These rats will eat me out of house and home if I am not careful," said the Little Old Woman. "I will catch them in a trap and drown them."

So the Little Old Woman went to the market and bought a large trap. She set the trap and baited it with bacon. Pretty soon she caught a rat.

"So far, so good," said the Little Old Woman. "Now I will drown this rat and catch another one."

But when the rat looked at her with his bright black eyes, she did not like to drown him.

"Poor thing, he looks hungry," she thought. "I will give him a bit of corn before I drown him."

After the rat had eaten the corn, he frisked about in

the trap. Then he curled himself up and sat looking at the Little Old Woman with his bright black eyes.

"There is no hurry about drowning the rat," she said. "Besides, I shall be very busy with my baking today. I will drown him tomorrow."

The next morning the Little Old Woman said to herself:

"I must drown that rat today so I can set the trap to catch another one."

But when she went up to the trap, the rat sat up on his hind legs and looked at her with his bright black eyes. She did not like to drown him.

"I shall be very busy in my garden today," thought the Little Old Woman. "Perhaps I had better wait until tomorrow to drown the rat."

The next morning the Little Old Woman said to herself:

"Today I must surely drown that rat so I can set the trap to catch the rest of them. There are seven more rats to catch, and they are eating me out of house and home."

But when she went up to the trap, the rat looked at her with his bright black eyes. Then he sat up on his hind legs and sniffed at her fingers.

"I may as well feed him some corn before I drown him," said the Little Old Woman.

When she brought the corn, the rat ate out of her hand.

"This is a very friendly rat."

"This is a very friendly rat," she said to herself. "I cannot bear to drown him. Perhaps if I open the trap and let him loose, he will run away."

The Little Old Woman opened the trap and turned the rat loose. But the rat did not run away. He came close to her and sat up on his hind legs. He sniffed at her fingers and looked at her with his bright black eyes.

"How tame he is," said the Little Old Woman. "I will keep him for a pet. But I will catch the other rats and drown them."

She set the trap again and baited it with bacon. Pretty soon she caught another rat.

"Now I will drown this one and set the trap to catch another," she said.

But when he looked at her with his bright black eyes, she did not like to drown him either. Instead of drowning him, she fed him some corn.

Every morning she gave him corn, and in a few days he was just as tame as the first rat. Meanwhile, the other six rats were getting into the cupboard and eating her victuals. They were making nests in her bureau drawers. And they were gnawing holes in the bag of corn and carrying away the corn.

"Something will have to be done," said the Little Old Woman. "The six rats I have not caught are eating me out of house and home. But whenever I catch a rat, I cannot bear to drown him. It is high time I used my head."

So the Little Old Woman tied a wet towel around her forehead and sat down with her forefinger against her nose and closed her eyes.

She used her head and used her head, and it was not very long before she knew what to do.

"I will catch the rest of the rats, one by one," she said. "When they become tame, I will keep them for pets.

"Every day I will feed them corn so they will not eat my victuals. I will also fix them a nice box to sleep in, so they will not make nests in the bureau drawers."

The Little Old Woman caught the rest of the rats one by one. When they became tame she kept them for pets. At night they slept by the fire in the nice box she had fixed for them. Every morning when she gave them corn, the rats sat up on their hind legs and ate out of her hands.

"Rats make very fine pets," said the Little Old Woman. "How clever I was to tame them. I will have to buy a little extra corn now and again. But it is far better to have eight pet rats than to be eaten out of house and home by wild rats."

4. How She Kept Her Geese Warm

ONE cold winter night, the Little Old Woman was out in the barn putting her geese to bed. She gave them some corn and took off their little red coats. Then she brushed each little coat with a whisk-broom and carefully shook out the wrinkles.

As she was folding the coats in a neat pile, she thought:

"My poor geese must be very cold at night. I have my cozy fire and my feather bed. But they have not even a blanket to keep them warm."

After the geese had eaten their corn, they began to go to roost.

"Honk, honk!" said the big gander, and he hopped up on the roost.

"Honk, honk!" said the gray goose, and she hopped up on the roost.

"Honk, honk!" said all the other geese, and they hopped up on the roost.

Then the Little Old Woman closed the barn door and

The geese began to roost.

went into the house. When she went to bed, she lay awake worrying about the geese. After a while she said to herself:

"I cannot sleep a wink for thinking how cold the geese must be. I had better bring them in the house where it is warm."

So the Little Old Woman dressed herself and went out to the barn to fetch the geese. She shooed them off the roost and put on their little red coats. She picked up two geese, and tucking one under each arm, she carried them into the house.

Then she went out to the barn and picked up two more geese. She tucked one goose under each arm and carried them into the house.

When the Little Old Woman had brought all the geese into the house, she said to herself:

"Now I must get them ready for bed again."

She took off their little red coats and gave the geese some corn. Then she brushed each little coat with a whisk-broom and carefully shook out all the wrinkles.

As she was folding the coats in a neat pile, she thought:

"It was very clever of me to bring the geese into the house. Now they will be warm, and I shall be able to sleep."

Then the Little Old Woman undressed herself again and went to bed.

After the geese had eaten their corn, they began to roost.

"Honk, honk!" said the gander, and he hopped up on the foot of the Little Old Woman's bed.

"Honk, honk!" said the gray goose, and she hopped up on the foot of the Little Old Woman's bed.

"Honk, honk!" said all the other geese, and they tried to hop up on the foot of the Little Old Woman's bed.

But it was not a very big bed, and there was not enough room for all the geese to roost. They began to fight. They pushed and shoved each other. They hissed and squawked and flapped their wings.

All night long the geese pushed and shoved each other. All night long they hissed and squawked and flapped their wings.

They made so much noise that the Little Old Woman did not sleep a wink.

"This will never do," she said. "When they were in the barn, *I* did not sleep for thinking how cold they must be. When they are in the house, I cannot sleep because they make so much noise. Perhaps if I use my head, I shall know what to do."

The Little Old Woman tied a wet towel around her forehead. Then she sat down with her forefinger against her nose and shut her eyes.

She used her head and used her head, and after a while she knew what to do.

"I will move the roost into the house," she said. "The geese will have the cozy fire to keep them warm. Then I will move my bed out into the barn. My feather bed will keep me warm, and I will not be worrying about the geese. They will not keep me awake with their noise. I shall sleep very comfortably in the barn."

The Little Old Woman moved the roost into the house, and she moved her bed out into the barn.

When night came again, she brought the geese into the house. After she had fed them some corn, she took off their little red coats. Then they all hopped up on the roost, and the Little Old Woman went out to the barn to sleep.

Her feather bed kept her as warm as toast. She was not worried about the geese, because she knew that they were warm too. So she slept as sound as a top all night long.

5. How She Finished Her Red Muffler

ONE warm summer morning the Little Old Woman looked out of the door of her little yellow house. She said to herself:

"It is too hot to work in my soup garden today. I will sit down by the window and knit myself a red muffler."

So she took her yarn and knitting needles out of the bureau drawer and put on her spectacles. Then she sat ·down by the window and began to knit herself a red muffler.

Pretty soon the Little Old Woman's geese wanted to go swimming in a pond not far from the house. They went to the gate and flapped their wings.

"Honk, honk!" they said.

The Little Old Woman got up and put her yarn and knitting needles away in the drawer and took off her spectacles. She went out and opened the gate so the geese could go to the pond.

When all the geese were out of the yard, the Little Old Woman closed the gate and came back to the house.

She took her yarn and knitting needles out of the bureau drawer and put on her spectacles. Then she sat down by the window and went on knitting her red muffler.

She had hardly knitted a dozen stitches before the geese came back from the pond. They stood outside the gate flapping their wings and shaking the water off their backs.

"Honk, honk!" they said.

The Little Old Woman got up again. She put her yarn and knitting needles away in the bureau drawer

and took off her spectacles. She went out and opened the gate.

When all the geese were back in the yard, the Little Old Woman closed the gate and came back to the house. She took her yarn and knitting needles out of the drawer and put on her spectacles. Then she down by the window and went on knitting her red muffler.

She had hardly knitted a dozen stitches before the geese wanted to go swimming in the pond again. But the Little Old Woman had no sooner let them out of the gate before they wanted to come back in again.

"Dear me," said the Little Old Woman, "I am spending all my time letting the geese in and out of the gate. At this rate, I shall never get my red muffler done. I think I will use my head and find out what to do."

So she tied a wet towel around her head and sat down with her forefinger against her nose and shut her eyes.

She used her head and used her head, and after a while she found out what to do.

"I will saw two holes at the bottom of the gate," said the Little Old Woman. "When the geese want to go to the pond, they can crawl out through one hole. When they come back from the pond after their swim, they can crawl in through the other hole."

So the Little Old Woman fetched her saw and sawed two holes at the bottom of the gate. As she was coming back to the house, she thought:

"Now I will not have to go out to open the gate for

the geese. And I shall have my red muffler knitted in no
time. What a clever Old Woman I am!"

She took her yarn and knitting needles out of the
bureau drawer and put on her spectacles. Then she sat
down by the window and went on with her knitting.

Pretty soon the geese wanted to go swimming in the
pond. They went to the gate and flapped their wings.

"Honk, honk!" they said.

But the Little Old Woman did not get up. She sat by
the window, knitting her red muffler.

The geese flapped their wings again.

"Honk, honk!" they said.

The Little Old Woman paid no attention to them.

After a while, the old gander spied one of the holes in

the gate. He crawled through the hole and went to the pond. Soon the gray goose spied the hole in the gate, and she crawled through it and went to the pond. Before long, all the other geese spied the hole in the gate, and they crawled through it and went to the pond.

The Little Old Woman sat by the window knitting her red muffler. She had hardly knitted a dozen stitches before the geese came back from the pond.

"Now they will flap their wings and say, 'Honk, honk!'" said the Little Old Woman. "But I will not get up and open the gate. By and by they will find the other hole and crawl through it."

But the geese did not flap their wings and say, "Honk, honk!" And instead of looking for the other hole, every one of them crawled back in the same way they had crawled out.

"How silly the geese are!" said the Little Old Woman. "Here I have made two holes, and they only use one of them. I might have spared myself all the trouble of making the other hole."

All morning long, the Little Old Woman sat by the window and knitted her red muffler. All morning long, the geese crawled back and forth through the same hole in the gate.

At last the Little Old Woman finished the red muffler. But the geese were still crawling back and forth through the same hole in the gate.

"It was very clever of me to make two holes after all," said the Little Old Woman. "The geese will have that hole worn out in no time. When it is worn out, the other hole will come in very handy. What a clever Old Woman I am!"

6. How She Did Her Marketing

ONE day when the Little Old Woman was weeding her soup garden, the pack peddler came along crying his wares.

"Any tacks, laces, nutmeg graters, ribbons, mousetraps or buttons today?" he cried.

The Little Old Woman shook her head.

"No," she said. "I have no money to spare. It is all I can do to make both ends meet."

"Any hairpins, cooking pots, calico, button hooks, needles or spices?" he cried.

But the Little Old Woman shook her head.

"No," she said. "Today is market day, and I must save my money to buy meat and bread for my supper."

"How about a pair of magnifying spectacles?" asked the peddler.

"Magnifying spectacles!" exclaimed the Little Old Woman. "And what may they be?"

"They are a very useful kind of spectacles," the peddler explained. "When you wear them, everything looks twice as large as before."

"How about a pair of magnifying spectacles?"

"But what good are they?" asked the Little Old Woman. "Why should I want things to look twice as big as before?"

"That is easy to answer," the peddler replied. "The larger things are, the more plainly you can see them."

"I never happened to think of that before," said the Little Old Woman. "What you say is very true."

"Why not put the spectacles on, and see for yourself how large things look?" said the peddler.

"Well, I suppose it would do no harm to try them on," she said. "But, mind you, I have no money to buy them."

"Just as you say," said the peddler.

He opened his pack and took out the magnifying spectacles. The Little Old Woman put them on and looked at her soup garden. She could hardly believe her eyes. The cabbages looked twice as big. The tomatoes looked twice as big. Everything in the garden looked twice as big as it had before.

"How my vegetables have grown!" exclaimed the Little Old Woman. "And how plainly I can see them! These are very fine spectacles indeed."

"They are quite cheap, too," said the peddler. "If you should buy them, I am sure they would come in very handy."

"That is just what I was thinking," the Little Old Woman replied. "I will fetch you some money from my china teapot."

She hurried into the house and took some money from

out of her china teapot to pay for the spectacles.

After the peddler had gone, she said to herself:

"I should like to look at the soup garden through these spectacles again. But first I must go to market and buy some bread and meat for my supper."

As she was getting ready to go to market, she thought:

"I will take the spectacles with me and wear them while I am doing my marketing. I will be able to see more plainly, and I will get more for my money."

So the Little Old Woman put the magnifying spectacles in her market basket and took them with her. After she reached the market, she put on the spectacles so she could see more plainly. When she went to buy her bread, she said to the baker:

"What fine rolls you have today! They are nearly as large as a loaf of bread. One roll will be all I will need."

She bought one roll and put it in her market basket. Then she went to buy her meat.

"What fine chops you have today," she said to the butcher. "They are nearly as large as a whole roast. One chop will be all I will need."

So she bought one chop and put it in her market basket.

As the Little Old Woman was coming home from market, she said to herself:

"I have never bought so much bread and meat for so little money. These spectacles are very useful indeed."

When she was home again, she set about preparing her supper. She took the roll out of the market basket.

"This roll is too big for one meal," she thought. "I will cut off a piece and save the rest for tomorrow."

After she had cut off a piece of the roll and put the rest away, she took the chop out of her market basket.

"This chop is too big also," she thought. "I will cut off a piece and save the rest for tomorrow."

So she cut off a piece of the chop and put the rest of it away.

When she had prepared her supper, the Little Old Woman took off her magnifying spectacles. She put them away carefully, and then sat down to eat.

She looked at the piece of roll. It was no bigger than a thimble. She looked at the piece of chop. It was no bigger than a thimble either.

"Mercy!" cried the Little Old Woman. "What has happened to my supper? There is not enough left to feed a mouse!"

She began to look for the rest of her supper. She looked at her plate. She looked under her plate. But she did not find it. She looked on the table. She looked under the table. But she did not find the rest of her supper.

After she had looked everywhere, she said:

"This is very strange. Something seems to be wrong, and I must use my head to find out what it is."

So she tied a wet towel around her forehead and sat down with her forefinger against her nose and shut her eyes.

She used her head and used her head. Pretty soon she found out what to do.

"What a silly Old Woman I am!" she said. "How can I find my supper when I cannot see plainly? I must put on my magnifying spectacles."

The Little Old Woman got her magnifying spectacles and put them on. Then she came back to the table. She looked at her plate, and there she saw her supper as plainly as anything.

As she sat down to eat, she said to herself:

"It was very wise of me to put on my magnifying spectacles. Now I see my supper very plainly. And what a fine big supper it is, to be sure! I am afraid I shall not be able to eat half of it."

7. How She Rested Her Head

ALL the year round the Little Old Woman used her head to find out what to do.

One evening she said to herself, "How time does fly! It seems only yesterday that I made my geese their little red coats and plucked their feathers to make my feather bed. Now it is fall again.

"I have used my head so much this year that I think I will give it a rest."

So the Little Old Woman sat down in her rocking-chair to rest her head.

"The nights are growing colder," she thought. "I had better sit closer to the fireplace."

She got up and moved her chair closer to the fire-place and sat down again. She folded her arms across her apron and put her feet on her little footstool.

"A fireplace is nice and warm," she said to herself. "I must gather some wood tomorrow so I can make a fire. My fireplace will be even warmer when I build a fire in it. And besides, a fire is so cozy to look at.

"The evenings will be very long now. I shall have plenty of time to sit by my fire and think. I shall think about pleasant things for that will rest my head.

"I shall think how warm my geese are in their little red jackets. I shall think how comfortable my rats are in their little box.

"I shall think how comfortable I am in my feather bed.

"It will be very pleasant to sit by my fire and think how contented and happy we are, and all because I used my head."

All winter long the Little Old Woman lived comfortably in her little yellow house with her geese and her rats.

At night she slept in her bed in the barn. Her down comforter kept her as warm as toast.

The geese slept on their roost in the house. They were warm too. And the rats slept in their warm box near the stove.

During the long winter evenings, the Little Old Woman sat in her rocking-chair by the fireplace. Sometimes she popped bowls of popcorn over the embers for herself and for the geese and the rats. Sometimes she just sat quietly and rested her head.

When spring came, she said to herself:

"I have been resting my head all winter and it is very well rested indeed. I am rested too. Now I will begin to do my usual spring chores. As soon as they are done, I will be all ready to use my head again."

The Little Old Woman set about doing her usual spring chores.

First, she moved the geese's roost out of her house and put it back in the barn.

"The nights will be warm from now on and the geese will sleep very comfortably in the barn," she thought.

Next, she moved her bed out of the barn and put it back in the house.

"I will not need my down comforter until winter comes again," she said.

She put the down comforter away in her camphor chest, along with the geese's little red coats and her winter woolens.

"Now I must plant my soup garden," said the Little Old Woman.

She planted her soup garden with seeds of all kinds of vegetables to use in her soup. She planted carrot seeds, parsley seeds, turnip seeds, garlic seeds, and cabbage seeds.

She planted onion bulbs in her blue window boxes so the onions would be handy when she needed one in a hurry; and she planted the tulip bulbs in the soup garden so that travelers passing by could enjoy seeing the tulip blossoms.

Last of all, the Little Old Woman fetched a bucket of blue paint and a paint brush, and put a fresh coat of paint on the two blue window boxes, and on the neat blue fence around her house.

Then she said to herself:

"All my usual spring chores are done and now I am ready to use my head again whenever I wish."

8. How She Took Things Easy

ONE summer day the Little Old Woman got up bright and early. She fed her rats and geese and cleaned her house. Then she put on her sunbonnet and went out and tended her soup garden. She hoed and weeded her garden and watered it with her little sprinkling can. She pulled vegetables from the garden and some onions for her window boxes to put in her soup.

When the soup was cooking on the stove, the Little Old Woman said: "The sun is barely up and all my work is done. As I have a little time to spare, I will rest and take things easy."

The Little Old Woman sat down in her rocking chair with her feet on a footstool and a soft pillow behind her head. She folded her arms across her red checked apron and took things easy.

After a few minutes, she said: "I am enjoying taking things easy very much, but if I had someone to visit with me, I would enjoy it even more. What a pity that I have no neighbors with whom I might visit. When they came to see me and my rats and geese, I would give them some doughnuts and cider. And when I took my rats and geese to visit them, no doubt they would be pleased to do as much for us. But I have no neighbors, so there is no use thinking about that."

When the Little Old Woman had taken things easy for a while longer, she said: "How pleasant it would be if now and again, passers-by would stop at my door, so I could visit with them. Many people *pass* my door. In summer they stop to look at my tulips, and in winter they stop to look at the geese in their little red coats. But winter or summer no passers-by *stop* at my door. Perhaps if I put my mind to it, I can figure out the reason."

The Little Old Woman put her mind to it and pretty soon she figured out the reason no passers-by stopped at her door.

"People do not stop at my door because they cannot see it," she said. "In summer it is hidden behind the tall stalks of corn and the bean poles in my soup garden. In winter it is hidden behind the snow that drifts on my fence. While I am taking things easy, I must try to think up a way to keep my door from being hidden so passers-by will stop at it."

The Little Old Woman took things easy and tried to think up a way to keep her door from being hidden.

"I could tear down my fence," she thought. "If I tear down my fence, snow cannot drift upon it and hide my door in winter. But I would not like to part with my fence. I had better think up another way to keep my door from being hidden."

After the Little Old Woman thought a while longer, she said: "I could stop planting corn and string beans in my soup garden, so they would not hide my door in summer. But if I did that, I would have no string beans or corn to cook in my soup. Surely I can find a better way than that!"

The Little Old Woman kept on trying to think up ways to keep her door from being hidden. Finally, she said: "Thinking is getting me nowhere. It is high time I used my head and found out what to do."

The Little Old Woman tied a wet towel around her forehead and sat down with her forefinger against her nose and closed her eyes. She used her head and used her head and before long she found out what to do.

"I will move my door close to the road," she said. "Then passers-by will see it easily and stop to visit with me."

The Little Old Woman lifted the door off its hinges. She dragged the door through her soup garden and over the fence to a green field close by the road.

"It was very clever of me to think of moving my door," said the Little Old Woman. "Now I will stand it up so passers-by can see it."

The Little Old Woman stood the door up in the green field close to the road. The door stood up very well as long as she held it, but as soon as she let go it fell down.

The Little Old Woman hung the door on its hinges.

"I wonder why the door will not stand up," said the Little Old Woman. "When it was on its hinges it never fell, as far as I can recall. Perhaps I had better fetch the hinges and hang the door on them."

The Little Old Woman started back to her house to fetch the hinges. When she got there, she said: "Since the hinges are screwed to the door frame I may as well bring the frame along, too."

She sat down in her rocking chair and closed her eyes.

The Little Old Woman took a hammer from her toolbox and pulled the nails out of the door frame. She dragged the door frame through her soup garden and over the fence to the green field. She stood the door frame up close to the road.

"The door frame stands up very well," said the Little Old Woman. "Now, when I hang the door on the hinges, it will not fall down."

But when the Little Old Woman lifted up the door and hung it on the hinges, the door fell down and the door frame fell down.

"However can I make that door stand up?" the Little Old Woman asked herself. "I had better use my head and find out."

The Little Old Woman went back to her house. She tied a wet towel around her forehead and then she sat down with her forefinger against her nose and closed her eyes. She used her head for quite a while and then she found out how to make the door stand up.

"First, I will mark off a square in the green field," said the Little Old Woman. "In each corner of the square I will stick a tall bean pole. Across the tops of the bean poles I will nail four long strips of wood. I will nail the doorway under the strip of wood closest to the road. Then the doorway will be steady and when I hang the door on its hinges, it will not fall down."

The Little Old Woman gathered some stones and marked out a square in the green field: She fetched four bean poles from her soup garden and stuck one pole in each corner of the square. Next, she dragged four strips of wood from her lumber pile to the green field.

"It is more trouble to move a door than I expected," she thought, as she was nailing the strips of wood across the tops of the bean poles. "However, until I have someone to visit with me, I am glad to have something to do while I take things easy."

' When the Little Old Woman had nailed the four strips of wood on top of the bean poles, she lifted up the door frame and nailed it under the strip that was closest to the road.

"Now I will hang the door on the hinges screwed in the door frame and see what happens," said the Little Old Woman.

When the Little Old Woman lifted up the door and hung it on the hinges, nothing happened. The door frame did not fall down and the door did not fall down.

"So far so good," the Little Old Woman thought. "Next I will try the door and see if it opens easily."

The Little Old Woman tried the door and found that it opened very easily. "While I am about it, I may as well step inside," she thought.

The Little Old Woman stepped through the doorway, and found herself in a little square house with a bean pole stuck in each corner.

"This is a surprise," she exclaimed. "In moving the door, I hadn't planned to build a house. I am sure I will find it very handy to have two houses. Since this new house has no walls and no roof it will be nice and cool for any passers-by who stop to visit with me during the summer. To be sure, it may be a little drafty when the cold weather sets in, but I can worry about that when the time comes. Meanwhile, I will go back to my little yellow house and cook my supper."

The Little Old Woman went back to her little yellow house and cooked her supper. She said to herself: "To-day, I have learned two things that are well worth knowing. First, I learned that by moving my door I can build me a new house any time I need one. Second, I learned that taking things easy is not as restful as I thought it would be. I have been taking things easy since early morning and, I declare, I couldn't be any more tired if I had been hard at work the whole livelong day."

9. How She Saw the Circus Come to Town

ONE fine summer evening, the Little Old Woman said to herself:

"Tomorrow the circus is coming to town. I should like very much to see it, but I have no money for a ticket.

"However, if it is a fine day, I shall get up very early and see the circus wagons and animals as they come into the market place."

When the Little Old Woman had finished her evening chores, she sat down and began unraveling some old gray woolen stockings and rolling the yarn into balls to use for darning. Pretty soon she said to herself:

"I had better tie a red string on my finger so that I will not forget to wake up to see the circus come to town.

"But," she thought, "while I am sleeping my eyes will be shut. I will not be able to see the string, and it will not remind me to get up. I must think of something else.

"If I had a rooster he would start crowing and that

would wake me up," she said. "But I have no rooster and it is too late to go to market to buy one."

After the Little Old Woman had thought a little longer, she said:

"I might stay up all night, of course. Then I would surely be up in time to see the circus come to town. However, if I stay up all night, I shall be too sleepy to look at it.

"I suppose there is nothing to do but use my head to find out how to wake myself up in time to see the circus come to town."

So, the Little Old Woman put down her yarn, and tied a wet towel around her forehead. Then she sat down with her forefinger against her nose and shut her eyes.

She used her head, and used her head. At last she found out how to wake herself up in time to see the circus come to town.

"I will wet a piece of my gray yarn and tie one end of it around my toe," she said. "Then, I will tie the other end of it to the bedpost. When the yarn dries it will shrink. That will make it shorter and it will pull my toe. When it pulls my toe, it will wake me up."

Then the Little Old Woman went on unraveling stockings and winding the gray yarn into balls.

"I feel quite sure that I will wake up when the yarn shrinks and pulls my toe," she thought, "but just to be on the safe side, I think I will tie a piece of wet yarn on the tail of each of the rats, and tie the other end to a leg of the stove. When the yarn dries, it will shrink and pull their tails. They will wake up and start to squeal, and that will help to wake me up, too."

The Little Old Woman cut some pieces of yarn and wet them. She tied a piece on each rat's tail and tied the other end to a leg of the stove.

Then she said to herself:

"While I am about it, I may as well tie a piece of wet yarn on a leg of each of my geese. I will tie the other end to the roost. When the yarn dries it will shrink and pull on their legs. They will start honking and hissing and flapping their wings. That will surely wake me up."

The Little Old Woman cut some more pieces of yarn and wet them. She went out to the barn where the geese were roosting. She tied a piece of wet yarn on a leg of each goose, and tied the other end to the roost. Then the Little Old Woman came back into the house, and finished unraveling the woolen stockings and winding the yarn into balls for darning.

When she was ready to go to bed she tied a piece of wet yarn around her toe and she tied the other end to the bedpost. Then she blew out the lamp and went to sleep.

While the Little Old Woman and the rats and the geese were sleeping, the yarn was drying and shrinking. As the yarn shrank it became shorter. After a while, the yarn that was tied to the rats' tails became so short that it pulled their tails. The rats began to squeal. They squealed and squealed.

At the same time the yarn that was tied on the geese's legs became so short that it pulled on their legs. They began to hiss and honk and flap their wings.

And the piece of yarn tied around the Little Old Woman's toe became so short that it pulled on her toe.

When the rats squealed and the geese began to hiss and honk and flap their wings, and the yarn pulled on her toe, the Little Old Woman woke up.

"It is still dark," said the Little Old Woman, as she lighted her lamp. "I am up in plenty of time to see the circus come to town."

As soon as she was dressed, she took her scissors and cut the yarn off each rat's tail. She went out to the barn and cut the yarn off the leg of each goose. Then she fetched her lantern and a little stool and her umbrella and started off to see the circus come to town.

She walked and walked until she came to the market place. Pretty soon she heard a great noise. Wagon wheels came rumbling down the dark streets. Men shouted, and horses' hoofs came "plack-plack" on the cobblestones.

"The circus is coming," said the Little Old Woman. "I will sit down and watch it."

She sat down on her little stool and saw the circus drive in. She saw the big animal wagons. She saw the tigers, bears and lions looking out of the air-holes in their boarded-up cages. She saw the camels and she saw the big white circus horses and the little Shetland ponies.

She saw a circus clown driving a sleepy donkey.

She saw four elephants walking slowly into the market place. A man was leading them. The first elephant was resting the end of his trunk on the man's shoulder. Each of the other elephants was holding the tail of the elephant in front of him with his trunk.

She saw the big circus cook-wagons, carrying a stove and pots and pans. And last of all, she saw the circus men putting up the tent.

By the time the circus men had finished putting up the big tent, and had fed and watered all the animals, the sun was coming up. Other people began coming to the market place to see the circus.

Then the Little Old Woman said to herself:

"It was very clever of me to think of tying wet yarn on my toe, on the rats' tails, and on the geese's legs to remind me to get up early.

"I was the only one who got to the market place in time to see the circus drive in.

"But, as I have always said, what would be the good of my having a head if I did not use it?"

10. How She Made the Baby Elephant Happy

WHEN the Little Old Woman came in sight of her house, she saw something gray and round and fat running around her garden.

As she came near enough to get a good look at it, she saw that it was a baby elephant.

"Mercy on me!" she said. "This is a great day indeed. First, I see the circus come to town and now I find a baby elephant in my garden."

As she watched the baby elephant running about the garden, and pulling up carrots and cabbages and turnips with his trunk, she thought: "It is not often that I find an elephant eating my vegetables. Indeed, so far as I can recall, I have never seen one in my garden before.

"I wonder where he came from. I could use my head and find out, of course. But this is no time to use my head. The main thing is that he is here, and I must make him happy so that he will not run away."

The baby elephant kept running about the garden pulling up cabbages and carrots and turnips with his trunk and eating them.

"I do not need to worry about feeding him," said the Little Old Woman. "He is feeding himself very well. However, I must find him a house, so that he can have a roof over his head.

"He could live in my house," she thought. "Then he could have my roof over his head. But his feet are so big he might step on the rats.

"Or, he might live in the barn," she said. "Then he

could have the barn roof over his head. But, if I put him in the barn, he might step on the geese. I had better build him a little shed and then he will have his own roof over his head."

As soon as she had fed the geese and the rats, the Little Old Woman set to work building a shed for the baby elephant. When the shed was finished she coaxed him into it by feeding him peanuts. She nailed a board across the front of it so that he would stay inside. Then she began to weed her garden.

The baby elephant started running after her and dragging the shed with him.

"What a funny elephant," said the Little Old Woman. "He likes to move his shed around with him."

But the shed was not easy to move. The posts dragged on the ground and made the baby elephant stumble. He did not like this so he lifted up his trunk and squealed. He squealed and squealed.

"Dear me!" said the Little Old Woman. "It is very sad to hear a baby elephant squeal. I must use my head and try to figure out how he can move his shed around without stumbling."

The Little Old Woman went into the house, and tied a wet towel around her head. Then she sat down with her forefinger against her nose and shut her eyes.

She used her head and used her head. Before long she had figured out how the baby elephant could move his shed around without stumbling.

"I will put a wheel on the bottom of each post," she said. "Then he can move his shed around very easily."

The Little Old Woman took the wheels off the little wagon that she used for hauling firewood in the winter. She put a wheel on the bottom of each post of the baby elephant's shed.

Then she went on weeding her garden. The baby elephant started running after her. The posts did not drag on the ground and he moved the shed very easily.

"It was very clever of me to think of putting wheels on his shed," said the Little Old Woman. "Now he can move it wherever he wants to and he will not stumble."

All day the Little Old Woman pulled weeds out of her garden. All day, the baby elephant followed her and pulled up carrots and cabbages and turnips with his trunk and ate them.

When the geese went for their evening swim in the nearby pond, the baby elephant went with them. He waded into the pond and filled his trunk with water. He blew water over the top of his shed, and he blew water on the geese.

He was very happy.

After supper the Little Old Woman took her mending and sat down in her rocking-chair on the porch.

The baby elephant had come back from the pond. He was running about the garden, pulling up carrots and cabbages and turnips with his trunk and eating them.

"I like this baby elephant very much," said the Little

Old Woman. "However, I hope no more baby elephants come to live with me. I have no more wood to make sheds and they would have no roofs over their heads.

"Moreover, I would not have enough vegetables to feed them. As it is, this baby elephant will have eaten everything in the garden by morning. Then I shall have to use my head to find out how to feed him."

Just then the Little Old Woman heard a great noise in the distance. Wagon wheels were rumbling, men were shouting, and horses' hoofs were going "plack-plack" over the cobblestones.

"Dear me," said the Little Old Woman. "That must be the circus leaving town."

The baby elephant heard the noise, too. When the Little Old Woman went around to the back of her house where she could watch the circus going over the distant hill, the baby elephant went with her.

They watched the big animal wagons go over the hill. They watched the camels and they watched the big white circus horses, and the little Shetland ponies.

When the baby elephant saw the big elephants walking slowly over the hill, he dropped the carrot he was eating and his big ears started waving back and forth. Then he lifted up his trunk and squealed. He squealed and squealed and squealed.

One of the big elephants dropped the tail of the elephant in front of her. She lifted up her trunk, and rumbled as loud as thunder.

Before the Little Old Woman could wink her eye, the baby elephant started running in his little shed. When he reached the fence he did not stop. He broke right through the fence and kept on running. He reached the hill just as the big cook-wagon went over its top.

The baby elephant ran up the hill and in a few seconds he too disappeared over the top.

"Dear me," said the Little Old Woman, "I do believe the baby elephant belonged to the circus. The big elephant who rumbled so loudly must have been his mother. Now he has gone back to her and I have no baby elephant."

She went back to the porch and sat down in her rocking chair.

"I shall miss the baby elephant very much," she thought.

"However, perhaps it is just as well that he has gone back to his mother. If he ate as much every day as he did today, I would have to use my head very hard to find out how to feed him.

"I am glad that I made him a little shed so that he will always have a roof over his head. It is a very useful thing to know how to make a shed for an elephant. If ever I find another elephant in my garden, I will know just how to go about it.

"I am a very wise old woman indeed."

11. How She Kept Herself Cheerful

ON the morning after the baby elephant ran away in his little shed, the Little Old Woman said to herself:

"I am afraid that I shall be very sad without the baby elephant. I must keep myself busy all day, so that I will not have time to miss him. Then I will keep more cheerful."

After she had washed the dishes and put her house to rights, she began to plan what she would do to keep herself busy.

"I could spend the day mending the big hole that the baby elephant made in the fence," she thought. "But the hole in the fence would make me think of him and I would be sadder than ever.

"I believe I will look over my preserve cupboard and see if there is anything in the line of winter preserves that I need to make."

The Little Old Woman opened the cupboard where she kept the jars of fruit, and the crocks of pickles, and jams, and the glasses of jelly and the bottles of catsup that she preserved to use during the winter.

"I have plenty of canned fruit," she thought. "And I have plenty of pickles and sweet and sour relish. I have plenty of bottles of catsup and plenty of crocks of jam.

"However, I do believe I could use some more glasses of jelly. I will make one glass of each kind of jelly. It will take me a long while and I will not have time to feel sad."

The Little Old Woman went to market and bought enough red currants, and green gooseberries, and purple grapes, and rosy apples to make one glass of jelly of each kind.

Then she set to work making the jelly. When the four little saucepans of fruit were cooking on the stove, she said to herself:

"It was very clever of me to think of keeping myself busy by making jelly. Nothing cheers me more than the smell of fruit cooking. And a few extra glasses will always come in handy."

When the fruit was cooked and strained, the Little Old Woman went to fetch some glasses, into which to pour the jelly. She looked high and low, but she found that she had no empty jelly glasses.

"Dear me," she sighed, "I have extra crocks for pickles and extra stone jars for jam, and extra bottles for catsup, but I haven't an extra jelly glass in my house.

The four little saucepans were cooking on the stove.

"This is a fine mess I've gotten myself into. In a few minutes the jelly will begin to jell, and I shall not be able to pour it. I must use my head very quickly."

The Little Old Woman tied a wet towel around her head. Then she sat down with her forefinger against her nose and shut her eyes. She used her head very quickly.

"It is really wonderful how fast I can use my head when I have to," she thought. "I have used it no time at all and yet I have found out just what to do.

"I will pour the jelly into the catsup bottles."

The Little Old Woman took four catsup bottles and poured one kind of jelly into each bottle. When she had set the red currant jelly, and the green gooseberry jelly, and the purple grape jelly, and the rose-colored rosy apple jelly on the window sill to cool, she said:

"My jelly looks even prettier in bottles than it does in glasses. I wonder that no one has ever thought of using bottles for jelly before.

"Now I must feed my geese and my rats," she said. "Then it will be time to get my own supper. I have been so busy all day that I have not had much time to think about the baby elephant."

When the Little Old Woman was ready to sit down to eat, she took the bottle of currant jelly and tried to pour some of it on her plate. But the jelly did not pour.

"My jelly has jelled very nicely," she thought. "But now I wonder how I am going to get it out of the bottle."

The Little Old Woman turned the bottle upside down and shook it, but the jelly would not come out. Then she tried to put a spoon down the neck of the bottle. But try as she would, she could not get the jelly out of the bottle.

"Dear me!" she thought. "This is most annoying. Maybe I shouldn't have used my head quite so fast. Now I shall have to open one of my glasses of jelly for supper."

The Little Old Woman put the bottle of currant jelly back on the window sill and opened a glass of currant jelly instead. As she was spreading the currant jelly on her bread, she looked at the bottles of jelly on the window sill.

"How pretty the jelly is," she thought. "I am just as glad that I did put it in bottles. Even if I can't get it out, it is a comfort to know that, come what may, I shall never run out of jelly.

"And what is more, I have kept myself busy and cheerful all day. And I have missed the baby elephant scarcely at all. What a wonderfully clever old woman I am!"

12. How She Got Her Fortune Told

THE next morning, as soon as the Little Old Woman was through with her housework, she looked around to see what she had in the way of furniture to put in her new house. She found a couple of barrels that could be made into chairs and a soapbox that would do for a table.

The Little Old Woman fetched her toolbox. In a short time she had the barrels sawed into chairs, and had nailed four legs on the soapbox to make a table. One by one, she carried them across the soup garden and through the gate to the green field where her new house stood. She set the soapbox table in the middle of the grass floor and put one barrel chair on each side of it. Then she fetched a pitcher of cider, some mugs and a bowl of doughnuts and set them on the table.

"Now I will sit down and take things easy until some passer-by stops at my door," the Little Old Woman said.

She sat down in one of the barrel chairs and leaned her head against the back of it. She rested her feet on a big rock that happened to be on the grass floor of her new house. Then she folded her arms across her red checked apron and took things easy. Before long, the Little Old Woman heard a knock at the door. When she opened it, she saw a tall dark gypsy woman standing outside.

"Come in and sit down," said the Little Old Woman.

"Thank you," the gypsy woman said, and came in and sat down.

"Do help yourself to a doughnut and I will pour you a glass of cider," the Little Old Woman said.

The gypsy helped herself to a doughnut and took a mug of cider that the Little Old Woman poured for her.

"I am glad you stopped at my door," said the Little Old Woman. "I was hoping someone would."

"Do you live all alone?" the gypsy asked.

"That I do," said the Little Old Woman. "True, I have a flock of geese and a great many pet rats to keep me company. But as they cannot talk it is rather hard to visit with them."

"I can see that it would be," said the gypsy.

"Not so long ago, I was so busy with my work that I had no time to visit," said the Little Old Woman. "However, I am and always have been a great one for using my head, and finding out handy ways to do things. I have found out so many handy ways to do my work that it is done very quickly. Nowadays I have so much time to spare that often I am hard put to know what to do with it."

"If you will let me read your fortune, perhaps I can help you in finding ways to spend your spare time," said the gypsy woman.

"I have never had my fortune read," said the Little Old Woman. "How do you do it?"

"I read your fortune by looking into the palm of your hand," the gypsy told her. "When I have looked into it, I will tell you all the things you have done and all the things you are going to do."

"It will be kind of you to go to so much trouble," said the Little Old Woman. "Please begin."

"With pleasure," said the gypsy. "But before I begin you must cross my palm with a piece of silver, and give it to me. A silver half dollar will do."

The Little Old Woman shook her head. "That I cannot give you," she said. "I have only one silver half dollar and I must save it to buy chops and rolls when I go to market."

"Then cross my palm with a silver quarter and give it to me," the gypsy woman coaxed.

Again the Little Old Woman shook her head. "I cannot give you a silver quarter, either," she said. "I have only one silver quarter and I must save it to buy a new broom when I go to market."

"Then I cannot read your fortune," said the gypsy woman, and she got up and started to leave.

"Please don't go," begged the Little Old Woman. "If you will help yourself to doughnuts and cider while I do a little thinking, I am sure I can find a way to cross your palm with silver and still keep my money."

"Very well," said the gypsy and she sat down and helped herself to the doughnuts and cider.

The Little Old Woman did a little thinking and soon she found a way to cross the gypsy's palm with silver and still keep her money. "In my cupboard is an old silver teapot with the lid broken off," she told the gypsy. "As the lid is just the size of a silver quarter, perhaps you will let me cross your palm with it."

"The teapot lid will do very well," said the gypsy.

The Little Old Woman went to her little yellow house and fetched the teapot and the broken-off lid. She made a crisscross on the gypsy's palm with the lid and gave it to her. The gypsy put the lid in the pocket of her long many-colored skirt. "Now I will tell you all the things you have done," she said.

"I shall be very glad to hear about them," said the Little Old Woman.

The gypsy took the Little Old Woman's hand and looked into her palm. "I see that you live all alone," she said.

"That I do," said the Little Old Woman.

"And I see that you are, and always have been, a great one for using your head," the gypsy said.

"Indeed I am," replied the Little Old Woman.

"Moreover, I see that you have many pets," the gypsy said. "I see a flock of geese and a great many rats."

"Do you see *all* my geese and *all* my rats?" asked the Little Old Woman.

"Yes, I see them plainly," the gypsy told her.

"Do you see the baby elephant I once had, who ran away the same day he came to me?" she asked.

"Yes, I see him, too," said the gypsy woman.

"Is he still wearing the little house I made for him?" asked the Little Old Woman.

"Yes, he is," said the gypsy woman.

"You have told me the things I have done very well," said the Little Old Woman. "Now, will you be so good as to tell me the things I am going to do with my spare time?"

"With pleasure," said the gypsy. "But before I begin, you must cross my palm with another piece of silver."

"I am sorry but I have no piece of silver to give you," said the Little Old Woman.

"Then I cannot tell you the things you are going to do," the gypsy said, and she got up to leave.

"Please don't go," the Little Old Woman begged. "If you will only give me time to use my head, I am sure I can find a way out."

The gypsy looked at the silver teapot that the Little Old Woman had set on the soapbox table. "A teapot without a lid is of no use to you," she said. "Why don't you cross my palm with it?"

"Let me read your fortune," said the gypsy woman.

"The very thing!" exclaimed the Little Old Woman. "I declare, with a little practice you could learn to use your head as well as I do."

The Little Old Woman picked up the teapot and made a crisscross on the gypsy's palm with the spout. The gypsy put the teapot in the pocket of her long many-colored skirt. Then she took the Little Old Woman's hand.

"What do you see?" asked the Little Old Woman.

"I see that you are going to travel," said the gypsy woman.

"That is good news to be sure," said the Little Old Woman. "I have always wanted to travel and it will be a pleasant and useful way for me to spend my spare time. Can you see when I am going to set off on my travels?"

"Yes," said the gypsy, "I can see that you are going to set off sooner or later."

"I am glad to get that settled," said the Little Old Woman. "Knowing just when I leave will be a big help in making my plans."

"Of course it will," said the gypsy. "And now I must be on my way. Have you any question you would like to ask before I leave?"

"If it is not too much trouble, I should like to know where my travels will take me," said the Little Old Woman.

The gypsy took the Little Old Woman's hand. "Your

travels will take you here and there, up and down, on land, and to and fro on water," she said.

"Those are the very places I have always wanted to go," exclaimed the Little Old Woman. "Now that I know when I am going and where my travels will take me, I have only to get my rats and my geese and myself ready and we will be ready to set off."

"I wish you a pleasant trip," said the gypsy woman.

When the gypsy had gone on her way, the Little Old Woman hurried back to her little yellow house. As she set about getting herself and her pets ready to travel, she thought: "What a pleasant morning this has been! I have had the gypsy woman to visit with and by letting her look into my palm I have learned about all the things I have done. I have also learned that I am going to spend some of my spare time by traveling. Best of all, I have learned all these things without parting with my silver money. It was very clever of me to think of giving the gypsy woman the broken teapot instead of my money. I doubt if I could have found a better way out even if I had used my head."

13. How She Traveled on Land

THE Little Old Woman was busy getting ready to travel here and there, and up and down on land, and to and fro on water. She washed the rats' patchwork quilts and hung them to dry in the shade of an apple tree. She mended the little red coats of the geese and spread them to air on a mulberry bush. She looked over her clothes-press and sorted out mitts, mittens, aprons, dresses, mufflers and hug-me-tights suitable for traveling in all kinds of weather.

She packed the rats' patchwork quilts, the red coats of the geese and her own clothes in a green carpetbag. She packed a picnic basket with bread, cold cuts of veal, jam, pickles and jelly for her own lunch; and she packed her market basket with corn, apples and peanuts for lunch for the geese and rats.

"Next I must make harnesses for my rats and geese so they will not get lost from me when we are on our travels," said the Little Old Woman.

She fetched her sewing box and a big ball of red

carpet rags and made a red harness for each rat and each goose. When she had caught all the rats and all the geese and put their harnesses on them, she said: "Now I will take a last look around my house before I go."

The Little Old Woman took a last look around her kitchen. As she was looking at her wood stove, she thought: "How many fine kettles of soup I have cooked on my wood stove! I fear I shall sadly miss it when I am on my travels!"

The Little Old Woman took a last look around her parlor. As she was looking at her rocking chair by the fireplace, she thought: "How many pleasant evenings I have spent sitting close to the fire in my rocking chair! I fear I shall sadly miss my chair and my bright fire while I am on my travels."

Next, the Little Old Woman took a last look around her bedroom. As she looked at her bed with its goose-feather comforter, she thought: "It will be a long time before I have the pleasure of sleeping in my own bed with my own feather comforter to keep me warm! I fear I shall sadly miss them while I am on my travels."

The Little Old Woman kept on going around her house and taking a last look at things. All the time she was looking, she kept thinking how sadly she would miss this and that of her comforts. "Ah me," she sighed. "What with one thing and another I am beginning to think I would rather stay at home than go on my travels.

The Little Old Woman set off along the road.

But since the gypsy woman looked into my palm and saw that I was to travel, travel I must."

The Little Old Woman put on her Easter bonnet and her best lace mitts and fetched her big purple umbrella. She caught the rats and geese, one by one, and held them by their red harnesses. "Now I have only to pick up my baggage and off we will go," she said.

The Little Old Woman kept hold of the red harnesses with one hand and tried to pick up the green carpetbag, the two lunch baskets and her big purple umbrella with the other hand. She found she could pick up the two lunch baskets or she could pick up the green carpetbag and her big purple umbrella. But to save her, she couldn't pick up all her baggage with one hand.

"Dear me," she said, "I should have asked the gypsy woman to look into my palm and see how I was to lead my geese and carry all my baggage with only two hands. As it is, I shall have to try to figure it out for myself."

Holding fast to the red harnesses, the Little Old Woman tried to figure out how she could lead her geese and rats and carry all her baggage with only two hands. After she had tried and tried she figured out a way.

"I will tie the harnesses of the geese and rats to my apron strings," she said. "Then I will have one hand free to pick up the two lunch baskets and my other hand free to pick up the carpetbag and my big umbrella."

She tied the red harnesses of the geese and rats to her

apron strings and picked up the two lunch baskets with one hand and the carpetbag and her big umbrella with the other hand. With the rats and geese following behind her, she set off along the road that led up a steep hill. The lunch baskets were heavy, and the green carpetbag and her big purple umbrella were heavy. Moreover, the rats and geese did not want to follow behind the Little Old Woman. The rats squeaked and squealed and tried to pull her back down the hill. The geese hissed and squawked and tried to pull her back down the hill.

"What with carrying so much baggage and being pulled by my rats and geese, I am finding travel rather tiring," the Little Old Woman said to herself. When she got to the top of the hill, she was so tired and puffed, she set down her baggage and sat herself down on a flat rock.

"The gypsy woman said I was to travel, and travel I will," she sighed. "But gypsy woman or no gypsy woman, I cannot go on until I have rested and caught my breath."

After she had sat on the flat rock for a while, she said to herself: "I have caught my breath, but I am far from rested and besides, I am hungry. As my rats and geese must be hungry, too, we may as well eat our lunch before we go on."

The Little Old Woman untied the rats and geese from her apron strings and spread out their lunch under a big oak tree. The rats and geese began eating as fast as they could eat. "My poor rats and geese are so hungry, they will have their lunch eaten in no time," said the Little Old Woman. "But what I am to feed them for their supper is more than I know."

The Little Old Woman spread her bread, cold cuts of veal, jam, pickles and jelly out on the flat rock. "I am so hungry that I am sure I will have eaten all my lunch in no time," she thought. "But what I am to eat for supper is more than I know."

As the Little Old Woman was resting and eating, she looked back down into the valley where she lived. First she looked at her soup garden inside the blue fence. "What a fine soup garden I have!" she thought. "I wonder who will hoe and weed and water it and keep it fine for me while I am on my travels?"

Next she looked at her little yellow house. "How spick-and-span my little yellow house is!" the Little Old Woman thought. "I wonder who will keep it spick-and-span for me while I am on my travels?"

Last of all, she looked at the blue door on her new house close by the road. "How clever I was to move my blue door close to the road, so passers-by would stop to visit with me," she thought. "But if any passers-by stop at my door while I am on my travels, I wonder who will visit with them?"

The Little Old Woman sat looking down into the

valley where she lived. But although she wondered and
wondered, she couldn't tell who would tend her soup
garden and keep her house spick-and-span and visit with
passers-by for her while she was on her travels.

"What with being so tired and so worried about my
little yellow house, my soup garden and the passers-by,
I have no heart to go on," she said. "But I dare say the
gypsy woman would be quite put out if I turned back
after she went to so much trouble to help me spend my
spare time. So, tired and worried as I am, I must catch
my geese and rats, and on we will go."

The Little Old Woman went to the big oak tree to
catch her rats and geese. She looked under the tree, but
the rats and geese were not there. She looked up into the
tree, but the rats and geese were not there. She looked
behind the tree, and she looked around the tree, but the
rats and geese were not there. Finally, she looked down
the hill and there she saw her rats and geese. With their
red harnesses dragging behind them they were running
home as fast as they could run.

"What a bother!" the Little Old Woman cried.
"Now I shall have to turn back and fetch them before I
go on."

She picked up the empty lunch baskets with one
hand, and the green carpetbag and her big purple umbrella with the other hand, and hurried down the hill.
By the time she got to her little yellow house the rats

and the geese had crawled into the yard through the hole in the fence. When the Little Old Woman opened her gate they all came running to meet her.

"Honk, honk," said the geese and they flapped their wings.

"Squeak, squeak," said the rats and they sat up on their hind legs and sniffed at her fingers.

"Dear me, my rats and geese are hungry," said the Little Old Woman. "I had better give them their supper before we set off again." She fetched some corn and fed her rats and geese. Then she said: "As I am hungry, too, I will have a bowl of soup before we set off."

She made a fire in the wood stove and heated some soup. When she had eaten it and washed the bowl, she said: "I am very tired and I feel a bit chilled. I may as well rest and warm myself before we set off."

She put a match to the logs in her fireplace and sat close to it in her rocking chair. As she rested and warmed herself, she thought: "How cozy it is to sit in my own rocking chair beside my bright fire. If I had only myself to please I would keep right on sitting and forget about traveling, here and there, up and down on land, and to and fro on water. But the gypsy woman said I was to travel and I must please her, too. Maybe, if I use my head for all it is worth, I can find a way."

The Little Old Woman tied a wet towel around her forehead and sat down with her forefinger against her nose and closed her eyes. She used her head and used her head. After she had used her head for all it was worth, she said: "How foolish I was to worry about pleasing the gypsy woman. Now that I have used my head, I see that I have done little else but please her this livelong day. First off, the gypsy woman said I was to travel here and there. Since I was *here* when I set off this morning and *there* when I got to the top of the hill, I have pleased her in that.

"Then, the gypsy woman said I was to travel up and down. Goodness knows, I traveled *up* when I climbed the hill and I traveled *down* when I came back home. The gypsy also said I was to travel on land and I have traveled on land. In fact, I have had enough of traveling on land to last me a lifetime. As for traveling to and fro on water, it is true I have not yet pleased the gypsy woman in that. But, thanks to using my head, I see I have spent enough time pleasing other people for one day. Instead, I will keep right on sitting in my rocking chair beside my bright fire and pleasing myself."

14. How She Traveled on Water

NEXT morning the Little Old Woman said to herself: "Now that I have rested it is high time I began to think about traveling to and fro on water."

She did her housework and fed her rats and geese and tended her soup garden. Then she sat down and began to think about traveling to and fro on water. After a while she said: "To my mind, the best way to travel on water is in a boat. As I have no idea where to get one, I suppose I must use my head and find out."

The Little Old Woman tied a wet towel around her forehead and sat down with her forefinger against her nose and closed her eyes. She had just started using her head when the pack peddler came to her door, crying his wares.

"Any ribbons, flyswatters, bobbins, court plasters, calicos, mousetraps, skillets or treacle today," he cried.

"Not today," said the Little Old Woman. "But if you have something in the way of a boat, I might buy it and save myself the trouble of using my head."

"I have some fine toy boats," he said. "I have toy sailboats, tugboats, fishing boats, canal boats and pirate boats."

One by one he took the toy boats out of his bag and set them on the table. "They are very fine," said the Little Old Woman. "But I have no use for a toy boat."

"How about a gravy boat?" the pack peddler asked, and he took a blue china gravy boat out of his bag and set it on the table.

"It is very pretty," the Little Old Woman told him, "but I do not need a gravy boat."

"What kind of a boat *do* you need?" asked the pack peddler.

"I need a boat suitable for me and my geese and rats to use in traveling to and fro on water," said the Little Old Woman. "If you do not have such a boat, perhaps you can tell me where to find one."

"I have seen many boats in my time," said the pack peddler. "There was the big boat that brought me here from the old country, for one."

"Would you say it was big enough to hold me, my rats and geese, and all our baggage?" she asked.

"I would say it was big enough and more," the pack peddler replied.

"Good enough!" said the Little Old Woman. "And now, if you will be so kind as to fetch it here, I will gladly pay you for your trouble."

"That I cannot do," the pack peddler said, "for this

boat I speak of is far off on the shore of the ocean."

"But how are my rats and geese and I to travel on this boat if it cannot be fetched to us?" cried the Little Old Woman.

"That is easy to answer," said the pack peddler. "Since the boat cannot be fetched to you, you must take your rats and geese and baggage and travel on land until you get to the boat."

"No, thank you," the Little Old Woman said. "I have already had enough traveling here and there and up and down on land to last me a lifetime. Do you know of a boat nearer home?"

"In the willows on yonder river is a small rowboat that I use to ferry myself to and fro," said the pack peddler. "It is close at hand, and if it suits you, you are welcome to use it."

"A small rowboat close at hand will suit me very well," said the Little Old Woman. "It is good of you to let me use it."

"I am happy to be of service," the pack peddler said. "And now, I must bid you good morning and a pleasant voyage."

As soon as the pack peddler was gone, the Little Old Woman set about getting ready to travel to and fro on water. She packed the rats' patchwork quilts, the red coats of the geese and her own clothes in her green carpetbag. She packed her market basket with corn, apples and peanuts for the geese's lunch. And she packed a

picnic basket with bread, cold cuts of veal, jam, pickles
and jelly for her own lunch.

When all her packing was done, the Little Old Woman
put on her Easter bonnet and her best black lace mitts.
She caught the geese and rats, one by one, and put their
red harnesses on them. She tied the harnesses to her
apron strings and picked up the two lunch baskets with
one hand and the green carpetbag and big purple
umbrella with the other hand. With the rats and geese
following behind her, the Little Old Woman set off to

The peddler took the toy boats out of his bag.

the near-by river. In the willows, she found the pack peddler's rowboat.

"So far, so good," said the Little Old Woman. "I have only to get my rats and geese, our baggage and myself aboard and off we will go."

The Little Old Woman unfastened the harnesses of the rats and geese from her apron strings and tied them to the prow of the rowboat. Next, she got her baggage aboard, and last of all, she climbed into the rowboat and sat down. As she was untying the boat from a small willow tree, she said: "I will row us across the river and there we will have our lunch. When I have rowed us back again, we will have traveled to and fro on water as the gypsy woman said I should. Then my travels will be over and I can go back to my little yellow house and enjoy my home comforts in peace."

Meanwhile, the geese had jumped into the river and were swimming away from the boat as far as their red harnesses would let them. When the Little Old Woman tried to row, the oars splashed them and tangled in the red harnesses. The geese hissed and squawked and tried to break away from the boat. They tried so hard to break away from the boat that it began moving. Pulling the boat behind them, the geese started swimming down the river.

"It is very kind of the geese to pull the boat and save me the bother of rowing it," the Little Old Woman thought. "The only trouble is they are swimming *down* the river, and I want to travel to and fro, *across* the river. I had better stop them while I try to figure out a way to make them go where I want them to go."

The Little Old Woman grabbed hold of a willow branch and held fast to it while she tried to figure out a way to make the geese go where she wanted them to go. After she had figured and figured, she said: "I will fasten an apple to the end of a willow pole and dangle it over the heads of the geese. The geese will swim after the apple and it will be easy for me to make them go where I want them to go."

The Little Old Woman tied up the rowboat while she broke off a tall willow pole and fastened an apple on the end of it with a bent hairpin. "Since the geese are kind enough to pull the boat and save me the bother of rowing, I may as well leave the oars behind," she thought.

She lifted the oars out of the oar locks and hid them under the willows. Then she untied the boat and held the willow pole so that the apple dangled over the geese. The geese saw the apple and swam after it. The Little Old Woman pointed the willow pole toward a pine woods across the river, and swimming after it, the geese pulled the boat behind them.

"How clever I was to figure out a way to make the geese pull the boat across the river," said the Little Old

Woman. "Thus far I am finding traveling to and fro on water far more pleasant than traveling here and there and up and down on land."

Swimming after the apple, the geese pulled the rowboat straight across the river. When they got to the pine woods on the far side, the Little Old Woman put down the willow pole and climbed out of the boat. She rolled a rock on the end of the boat's rope and unloaded her baggage. Then she untied the rats and geese, and gave them their lunch.

As she was spreading out her own lunch under the pine trees, she thought: "What a pleasant place this is! As long as I am here I may as well have a quick look around, and see what there is to see."

After the Little Old Woman had eaten her bread, cold cuts of veal, jam, pickles and jelly, she got up and had a quick look around. On the ground under the trees, she saw heaps of pine cones and pine knots.

"These pine cones and pine knots would burn brightly in my fireplace," she said. "I will take some of them home in my market basket." She filled her market basket with pine cones and pine knots and put it in the rowboat.

The Little Old Woman took another quick look around. In a sunny field, she saw many stalks of goldenrod and Queen Anne's lace.

"These flowers would brighten my house," she said. "I will pick some of them to take home with me." She picked some goldenrod and Queen Anne's lace and put them in the rowboat.

Once more the Little Old Woman had a quick look around her. Growing by a zigzag fence she saw some thimbleberry bushes covered with ripe berries.

"These thimbleberries would make me a fine batch of jam," she said. "I will fill my picnic basket with them to take home with me."

She fetched her picnic basket and began picking the

She filled her basket with pine cones.

thimbleberries. By the time she had filled the basket, the sun was beginning to set.

"How time flies," exclaimed the Little Old Woman. "I never would have believed it could take me so long to have a quick look around. If I am to get home before dark I must make ready to set off at once."

The Little Old Woman made ready to set off. One by one, she caught her rats and geese and tied them to the prow of the boat. Then, she climbed into the boat and jerked its rope out from under the big rock. The geese began swimming away from the shore and pulling the boat behind them.

"Now I will hold the willow pole so that the apple will dangle over their heads," said the Little Old Woman. "The geese will swim after the apple and we will be home in no time."

But when the Little Old Woman picked up the willow pole, she saw that there was no apple dangling from the end of it.

"Mercy on me," cried the Little Old Woman, "the geese have eaten the apple and I have nothing to dangle over their heads to make them pull the boat home. This is a fine mess I've gotten myself into, and to get out of it I shall have to use my head as I've never used it before."

The Little Old Woman dipped her pocket handkerchief into the water and tied it around her forehead. She put her forefinger against her nose and closed her eyes. Then she set to work using her head as she had never used it before. Because she had been in the warm sun all day the Little Old Woman was sleepy. The harder she used her head the sleepier she got, and soon she was fast asleep. While the Little Old Woman slept, the geese kept on swimming and pulling the rowboat behind them. Pretty soon, the rowboat gave such a bump that the Little Old Woman woke up.

"Dear me, I must have dozed off and goodness only knows where the geese have pulled the boat!" exclaimed the Little Old Woman. "I could open my eyes and find out, of course, but I will not take time for that now. Instead, I must use my head and find a way to make the geese pull the boat home."

Keeping her eyes tightly closed, the Little Old Woman put her forefinger to her nose. She was just about to use her head when the rowboat gave another bump. The Little Old Woman went on trying to use her head and the rowboat kept on bumping. At the same time the geese began hissing and honking and the rats began squeaking and squealing.

"What with wondering where the geese have pulled the boat and what is bumping it and why the rats and geese are making so much noise, I'm afraid I am not using my head very well," said the Little Old Woman. "Perhaps I had better open my eyes and see what is what."

The Little Old Woman opened her eyes. The first thing she saw was that the geese had pulled the rowboat across the river to the very spot where she had found it hidden in the willows. The next thing she saw was that the geese had waded out of the water and were trying to break away from the boat. They were trying so hard to break away, they were bumping the boat on the shore.

"However did the geese know enough to come home?" the Little Old Woman asked herself. "For the life of me, I cannot remember using my head and finding out a way to make them do it!"

She climbed out of the boat and fastened it to the willow tree. Then she untied the geese and rats and picked up her baggage. With their red harnesses dragging after them, the rats and geese ran home as fast as they could run. As she followed them, the Little Old Woman kept asking herself how the geese knew enough to come home. When she opened her gate the rats and geese ran to meet her.

"Squeak, squeak," said the rats and they sat on their hind legs and sniffed at her fingers.

"Honk, honk," said the geese and they flapped their wings. Then the Little Old Woman knew why the geese had known enough to come home. "The geese came home because they were hungry and wanted their supper," she said. "All I needed to do, was to sit in the boat and let them pull it behind them. And as I did just that, it is as plain as day that I was using my head even when I slept."

The Little Old Woman fed her geese and rats and

cooked her own supper. As she was eating, she thought: "This has been a great day indeed. I have traveled to and fro on water, and thanks to the geese pulling the boat, I was spared the bother of rowing. I have brought home many pine cones and pine knots for my fire, a bouquet to brighten my house and enough thimble-berries to make me a fine batch of jam. And, best of all, by dozing off in the boat, I have found out that I can use my head when I am sound asleep every bit as well as when I am awake."

15. How She Saved Her Pennies

WHEN the hot days were over and the mornings began to be frosty, the Little Old Woman began getting ready for winter.

She dug up the tulip bulbs from the garden and laid them in a tin box. She put the box in a safe dry place near the chimney.

She wrapped her Easter bonnet in tissue paper and put it away in a box on her closet shelf.

She brought a load of wood from the market to burn in the kitchen stove, and she gathered kindling wood and pine cones to burn in the fireplace.

Then she said to herself:

"Now I must look over the winter woolens in my camphor chest to be sure there are no moth holes in them."

Then the Little Old Woman looked over all the woolens in her camphor chest. First she looked over her red woolen muffler. It had no moth holes in it, so she put it aside.

Then she looked over her down comforter. It had no moth holes in it. She put it aside and went on looking over her winter woolens. She looked over her heavy coat and her knitted stockings, and her winter flannels. None of them had moth holes in them, so she put them all aside.

Finally she looked over the geese's little red coats. They had no moth holes in them, but nearly all of the brass buttons on the coats were missing. Some coats had only one button on them and the other coats had no buttons at all.

"The geese are very careless," said the Little Old Woman. "They have lost nearly all the brass buttons that I sewed on their coats. Their coats will not stay on without buttons to fasten them. I must sort out the buttons in my big button-bag. Then I will see what I have in the way of buttons to replace the ones they have lost."

The Little Old Woman fetched her button-bag and began sorting buttons. She sorted bone buttons and pearl buttons and cloth-covered buttons. She sorted wooden buttons and colored glass buttons and some very fine tortoise-shell buttons. But when all the buttons were sorted, she found she had nothing at all in the way of brass buttons.

"Dear me!" she thought. "I have so many kinds of buttons but none of them will do to sew on the geese's little red coats. No buttons look so well on red as brass buttons. I shall have to buy some new brass buttons from the pack peddler when he comes today. That will cost me many a pretty penny."

The Little Old Woman took her china teapot down from the cupboard and counted out all her pennies. Then she stacked the pennies in neat piles on the table so they would be handy when the pack peddler came.

"While I am waiting, I may as well put the winter woolens to air," she said.

She gathered up her red muffler and down comforter and heavy coat and knitted stockings and winter flannels and the geese's little red coats. Then she went out to hang them on the clothesline in the soup garden.

She was just hanging up the last of the little red coats when the pack peddler came in through the gate.

"Good morning," he said.

"Good morning to you," said the Little Old Woman.

"Do you want to buy any shoe-strings, can-openers, kid-curlers, pie-pans, toothache drops, or fly-swatters today?" asked the pack peddler.

"No, I don't," the Little Old Woman replied. "However, will you please step into the house? I'd like to see what you have in the way of brass buttons suitable for geese's coats."

"Very well," said the pack peddler, and he followed her into the house. He opened his bag and took out everything he had in the way of brass buttons.

The Little Old Woman looked at all the brass buttons. She looked at large brass buttons, she looked at medium-sized brass buttons, she looked at small brass buttons. Finally, she found some brass buttons that were just the size she wanted.

"How much are these buttons?" she asked.

"They are a very great bargain," the pack peddler replied. "I am selling them at two for a penny."

"That is a lot of money," said the Little Old Woman.

"They are very fine buttons," the pack peddler replied, "you would do well to buy them."

The Little Old Woman looked at the brass buttons. Then she looked at the bright pennies stacked in neat piles on her table. She shook her head.

"They are very nice buttons, but I cannot make up my mind to part with so many pennies. Suppose you stop in on your way back, and I will let you know what I decide."

After the pack peddler was gone the Little Old Woman sat looking at the pennies.

"Dear me," she said, "the geese must have brass buttons to fasten their coats. Yet I cannot bear to part with my pennies. Is there no way I can get buttons for their coats and still keep my pennies? I think I'll use my head and see if I can find out how it can be done."

The Little Old Woman tied a wet towel around her forehead. Then she sat down with her forefinger against her nose and shut her eyes.

She used her head and used her head and pretty soon she found out how it could be done.

"I will use the pennies for buttons and sew them on the coats," she said. Then the geese will have buttons to fasten their coats and I shall still have my pennies."

Just then the pack peddler came back to the door.

"Well, have you decided to buy the brass buttons?" he asked.

"No, indeed," said the Little Old Woman. "I have used my head and decided to save my pennies.

"However, if you have anything in your bag that is useful for making holes in pennies, I shall be glad to look at it."

"I have small hand drills," said the pack peddler, taking one out of his bag. "I am selling them for a dollar apiece."

"The very thing," said the Little Old Woman. She fetched the dollar from her china teapot and bought the hand drill.

When the pack peddler had gone, the Little Old Woman drilled two holes in each of the pennies with the hand drill. Then she brought the geese's little red coats in from the line, and sewed on the pennies in place of buttons. She said to herself:

"It was very clever of me to think of using the pennies for buttons. Now the geese have buttons to fasten their coats, and I have saved my pennies.

"I like my pennies on the geese's coats very much. I can see them better than when they were in my china teapot. From now on I shall probably save all my pennies

"I have used my head and decided to save my pennies."

by sewing them on the geese's coats. In that case it is a good thing that I bought the hand drill to make holes in the pennies.

"What a wise old woman I am. Some day, no doubt, I shall be as rich as I am wise."

16. How She Brightened Her Home

ONE bitter cold morning the Little Old Woman took her wagon to the woods for logs and kindling to burn in her fireplace. As she was gathering the wood, she saw a red berry shrub growing close by.

"While I am about it," she thought, "I will pick a bouquet of red berries to brighten my house."

When she had filled her wagon with firewood and picked a bouquet of red berries, she started home. On her way, she came across a crow lying on the ground.

"The poor bird is all but dead with cold and hunger," said the Little Old Woman. "I will take him home and thaw him out. Then I will feed him and set him free."

She picked up the crow and brought him home, too. She put the red berries in a blue bowl on the mantelpiece and set about thawing out the crow. She lined a pasteboard box with cotton batting and laid the crow in it. She set the box on a bench close to the fire and set a saucer of corn beside it. Then she sat down with her mending and waited for the crow to thaw out. Pretty soon the crow began to flutter his wings and caw. "He is thawing out very well," said the Little Old Woman. "As soon as I have finished my mending, I will feed him and set him free."

But before the Little Old Woman had her mending finished, the crow fluttered his wings and hopped out of the box. "Caw, caw," he said, and started eating the corn.

"Since he is eating by himself I will not have to feed him," said the Little Old Woman. "Instead, I will go on with my mending."

When the crow had eaten his fill, he flew up on the mantelpiece, and started to eat the red berries.

The Little Old Woman jumped up. "Dear me, he is spoiling my bouquet," she said. "Now that he has thawed out and eaten his fill, it is high time that I set him free."

She opened the door and shooed out the crow. But before she had time to shut the door, the crow flew back into the house. Again the Little Old Woman opened the door and shooed out the crow, and again, before she had time to close the door, the crow flew back into the house.

"This must be a tame crow who is not used to making his own way in the world," said the Little Old Woman. "It would be cruel to turn a tame crow out of my house in the dead of winter. I see I shall have to keep him for a pet."

The crow lighted on the arm of her chair and started eating the berries.

Meanwhile the crow had lighted on the mantelpiece and was busily eating the red berries. As the Little Old Woman shooed the crow off the mantel, she thought: "I shall enjoy having a pet crow very much. But I should also enjoy having a bouquet of red berries to brighten my house. Perhaps if I sit down and think, I can find a way to keep him from eating the berries."

The Little Old Woman sat down but, before she had a chance to think, the crow flew back to the mantelpiece and started eating berries. The Little Old Woman jumped up and shooed him away. She had no more than sat down before the crow was back eating the red berries.

"This crow keeps me so busy jumping up and down, I have no time to think," the Little Old Woman said, as she jumped up and shooed the crow off the mantelpiece. "I had better keep the bowl of red berries by me until I have found a way to keep him from eating them."

The Little Old Woman picked up the bowl of red berries and sat down with it. The crow lighted on the arm of her chair and started eating the berries. Holding the bowl of red berries in one hand and shooing away the crow with the other, the Little Old Woman tried to think of a way to keep the crow from eating the berries.

"I could keep right on holding the bowl of red berries in one hand and shooing away the crow with my other hand," she thought. "The only trouble is that I might find it a bother to carry the bowl and shoo the crow when I am doing my housework. I could turn my wash boiler upside down and set the bowl of red berries under it," she thought. "But if I did that, I could not see the berries and they would not brighten my house."

After the Little Old Woman had spent a little more time shooing away the crow and thinking, she said: "The best way to keep this crow away from the berries will be to make a cage and put him in it."

The Little Old Woman jumped up, and, carrying the bowl of berries with her, she fetched some branches from her grapevine and a lid from a large round cheese box. She put the bowl of red berries, the grapevines and cheese box lid on the table and set to work making a cage.

All the time the Little Old Woman was making the cage the crow kept lighting on the table and trying to eat the red berries. All the time the Little Old Woman was making the cage, she had to keep shooing away the crow. She wove the grapevine in and out to make the top of the cage and she used the round cheese box lid for the bottom of the cage. She cut a square hole in the cage and wove a little door to hang over it. She fastened a small teacup filled with corn on one side of the cage and a small teacup filled with fresh water on the other side. She put a twig of kindling wood across the middle of the cage for a perch. Last of all, she made a little swing out of a clothes pin and a bit of string.

As she was shooing away the crow, and hanging the

swing in the cage, she said to herself: "How happy the crow will be in this fine cage with a perch and a swing to amuse him, and corn and water handy for him to eat and drink. How glad I shall be to be done shooing him away."

When the Little Old Woman put the crow in the cage and shut the door, the crow began beating his wings against the sides of the cage and squawking, "Caw caw."

"Mercy me!" cried the Little Old Woman. "Can it be that the crow does not like his cage after I have worked so hard to make it for him?"

The crow beat his wings against the cage harder and harder, and squawked louder and louder. "He will hurt himself if he keeps on beating his wings against the cage," said the Little Old Woman. "I had better let him out."

When the Little Old Woman let the crow out, he flew to the table and started eating the red berries. The Little Old Woman shooed him away and picked up the bowl of berries.

"I have wasted my whole morning trying to keep the crow from eating the berries and all for nothing," she said. "Now I will sit down and use my head as I should have done in the first place."

The Little Old Woman tied a wet towel around her forehead and sat down with the bowl of red berries. She put her forefinger against her nose and closed her

The Little Old Woman sat down and took things easy.

eyes. Flapping her elbows up and down to shoo away
the crow, she began using her head. She flapped her
elbows up and down and used her head, and flapped her
elbows up and down and used her head. When she had
flapped her elbows up and down and used her head for
quite a while, she found a way to keep the crow from
the red berries.

"It is so simple, that if I hadn't had to shoo away the
crow so much I wouldn't have had to use my head," she
cried. "I will put the bowl of red berries in the cage.
They will not mind being in the cage and the crow will
not be able to get at them."

The Little Old Woman jumped up and put the bowl of red berries in the cage and hung it in the sunny window. The crow flew after her and lighted on the cage. He pecked at the cage, but when he found he could not get at the red berries he flew to the mantelpiece and hid his head under his wing.

"I do believe the crow is going to sleep," said the Little Old Woman. "If he is half as tired of being shooed as I am tired of shooing him, I am sure he needs a little nap. While he is settled down, it will do me no harm to take things easy for a few minutes."

The Little Old Woman sat down in her rocking chair with her feet on a footstool and a soft pillow behind her back. She folded her arms across her red checked apron and took things easy. While she was taking things easy, she looked at the mantelpiece where the crow was asleep.

"I like this crow very much," she thought, "and now that he cannot eat the red berries he will make a fine pet." Then she looked at the cage hanging in the sunny window with the red berries in it.

"There is nothing like a bowl of red berries to brighten up one's house in winter," she thought. "And how clever it was of me to think of putting the red berries in the cage instead of the crow. But be it spring, summer, autumn or winter, there never was an old woman more clever than I. And, as I have said and always will say, 'It all comes of using my head!'"

17. How She Put Up Her Christmas Tree

ONE bright winter morning just before Christmas, the Little Old Woman began planning how she would make her rats and geese happy on Christmas day.

"My poor geese and my poor rats have no stockings to hang up at the fireplace," she sighed. "But at least they shall have the biggest and finest Christmas tree that I can find for them."

After she had washed the breakfast dishes and put the house to rights, the Little Old Woman got ready to go for a Christmas tree. She put on her warmest coat and her warmest bonnet and her fur-lined overshoes. She tied her red woolen muffler around her neck and drew on her thick red mittens.

Then she took her hatchet and set off across the snowy field to find a Christmas tree for her pets.

Very soon she came to a place where a great many Christmas trees were growing. There were tall thin trees, and short fat trees and medium-sized trees. There were straight trees and crooked trees and little straggly trees.

She came into the house dragging the tree behind her.

There were so many Christmas trees that the Little Old Woman hardly knew which one to choose.

First she decided to take a short fat tree. Next, she saw a tall thin tree that struck her fancy. Then she made up her mind to take a very crooked tree with almost no branches at all. She felt so sorry for it because she was quite sure no one else would choose it.

But finally she came to a little clearing, and there, standing all by itself, was the very finest tree of all. It was tall and straight and it was just the shape of a big green Christmas bell.

The minute the Little Old Woman laid eyes on it, she knew it was just the tree she wanted, so she began to chop it down with her hatchet. She chopped and chopped until the tree fell down. Then she dragged it across the snowy field to her own door.

When she came into the house dragging the tree behind her, the rats and geese did not know what to make of it. They were very much frightened. The rats began squealing and scampering into their holes. The geese began hissing and flapping their wings.

"They are not used to seeing a tree lying down," said the Little Old Woman. "However, when I put it up, I am sure they will like it very much."

But when the Little Old Woman tried to put up the tree, she found it was too tall to fit in the room.

"Dear me," she sighed, "how am I going to put up a Christmas tree for my rats and geese, if it is too tall to fit in my house?

"I might buy a new house," she thought, "but that would cost a lot of money.

"Or, of course, I could trim the tree and leave it lying on the floor," she thought. "But the rats and geese do not seem to like the tree lying on the floor.

"Perhaps," she decided, "it would be better to take this tree back to the woods and chop down another tree. If the other tree did not fit the house, I could take *it* back to the woods and get still another tree.

"I could keep right on chopping down trees and dragging them back and forth until I found one that was the right size to fit in my house."

But after the Little Old Woman had thought about this for a while longer, she said:

"It would be a lot of work to chop down so many trees and drag them back and forth. As it is, I am so tired that I believe I will just rest a bit. While I am resting I will use my head and maybe I will find out how to make this tree fit my house."

So the Little Old Woman rested and used her head.

First she tied a wet towel around it and then she sat down with her forefinger against her nose and shut her eyes.

She used her head and used her head and used her head. By the time she was rested she knew just what to do.

"I will chop a hole in the floor," she said. "Then I will stand the trunk of the tree in the hole. That will give the tree more room and it will fit in the house. How easy it is for me to find out what to do when I use my head!"

When the Little Old Woman had chopped a hole in the floor, she tried to stand the trunk of the tree in the hole. But the tree was still a little bit too tall to fit in the house.

"What a bother," she sighed. "I am getting very tired of trying to make this tree fit into my house. My head is getting very tired too. However, I suppose I shall have to use it again and find out what to do next."

So the Little Old Woman tied a wet towel around her head and sat down with her forefinger against her nose and shut her eyes. She had hardly used her head a minute before she knew what to do next.

"What a silly old woman I am," she cried. "If I had not been so tired, I would have known what to do without using my head.

"I must chop a hole in the roof. The top of the tree will stick out through the hole and then the tree will fit in the house very nicely."

The Little Old Woman fetched a ladder from the barn and placed it against the house. She climbed up the ladder and chopped a hole in the roof. Then she came back in the house to put up her Christmas tree.

She stood the trunk of the tree in the hole in the floor. The top of the tree stuck out through the hole in the roof, and at last the tree fitted into the house.

By now, the rats and the geese had gotten over being

frightened at the tree. The rats stopped squealing and peeked out of their holes to look at it. The geese stopped hissing and flapping their wings. They began walking around the tree. Some of the geese flew into the tree to roost.

"It is very lucky that I used my head and figured out a way to put up the tree," said the Little Old Woman. "My rats and my geese like their Christmas tree very much, now that it is standing up.

"It was also a fine idea to chop holes in the floor and roof. I shall put them to good use when Christmas is over and I take down the tree.

"The hole in the floor will be very handy to brush dirt into when I am sweeping. The hole in the roof will come in handy too. Whenever it rains I can set a bucket under the hole to catch rain water. Then I will not have to go out in the rain to carry water from the well.

"I am using my head better every day and I do believe there is not another old woman alive who is as wise and clever as I am."

18. How She Trimmed Her Tree

On the day before Christmas, the Little Old Woman set about trimming the Christmas tree which she had put up for her geese and her rats.

She popped two big bowls of popcorn and strung it on long strings. She strung long strings of cranberries, and she strung long strings of yellow crabapples. She made balls of green cheese to hang on the tree for her rats. And she made cornucopias of blue paper and filled them with peanuts to hang on the tree for her geese.

Last of all, she made a big gold paper star to hang on the very top of the tree.

When the Little Old Woman had everything ready she put the rats and the geese out of the house so they would not be in her way. Then she began trimming the tree.

She hung long strings of popcorn and red cranberries and yellow crabapples on the low branches. She climbed on a chair and hung long strings of popcorn and red cranberries and yellow crabapples on the high branches. All over the tree she hung little balls of green cheese and the blue cornucopias filled with peanuts.

119

She looked at the star on the Christmas tree.

"Now, I must tie the gold paper star on the very top of the tree," said the Little Old Woman. "As the top of the tree is sticking through the hole in the roof, I must go out and climb up the ladder to tie the star on it."

The Little Old Woman took the star and climbed up on the roof. When she had tied the star on the top of the tree, she thought:

"The star looks very pretty on the roof. To be sure, I cannot see it when I am in the house. However, it will be nice to know it is up here. And when I *do* wish to see it, it will be no trouble to climb up on the roof again."

When the Little Old Woman had climbed down from the roof, she said:

"Now, I will see how the geese and the rats like the trimming on the tree."

She opened the door and let the geese and the rats into the house. When they saw the tree, they were very happy.

"Honk, honk!" said the geese and they all flew into the tree.

"Squeak, squeak!" said the rats and they all ran up the tree.

"My geese and my rats like the trimming on the tree very much," said the Little Old Woman. "I am glad that I went to so much pains to please them."

Then the geese and the rats began to eat the trimming. Each of the geese began trying to eat all the trimming.

Each of the rats began trying to eat all the trimming. They started to fight.

The geese hissed and squawked and flapped their wings. They pecked each other and they pecked the rats.

The rats squeaked and squealed. They bit each other and they bit the geese.

The geese and the rats tore all the long strips of popcorn and red cranberries and yellow crabapples off the tree. They knocked down the balls of green cheese and they knocked down the blue cornucopias and spilled the peanuts. In a few minutes there was no trimming on the tree except the gold star on the roof, which they could not see.

"Mercy on us," said the Little Old Woman. "My geese and my rats liked the trimming too well. They have eaten it all up."

After the geese and the rats had eaten all the trimming, they stopped fighting. Pretty soon the geese went out for a walk and the rats crawled into their box to take a nap.

"Now what am I to use for trimming on their tree?" the Little Old Woman thought. "I am afraid I shall have to use my head long and hard to find that out!"

The Little Old Woman tied a wet towel around her head. Then she sat down with her forefinger against her nose and shut her eyes.

She used her head and used her head and used her

The geese and the rats ate all the trimmings.

head. After she had used her head long and hard she found out how to trim her tree.

"There is no use making any more trimming for the tree," she said. "The geese and the rats would only eat it. Instead, I will let the rats and the geese trim the tree themselves.

"The geese roost on the branches anyway. They will make very pretty trimming, roosting on the tree in their little coats.

"I will brighten up the rats a bit, and they will make pretty trimming, too."

When the rats had finished their nap, the Little Old Woman brightened them up. She took some red ribbon from her scrapbag and some blue and red and yellow beads from her work-box. She tied a little string of blue and red and yellow beads around the neck of each rat. She tied a bow of bright red ribbon on the tail of each rat.

After all the rats were brightened up, the Little Old Woman rubbed strong cheese on the branches of the tree.

When the rats smelled the cheese, they ran up into the tree and began gnawing the branches. They all stayed in the tree gnawing and gnawing the branches.

After a while the geese came in from their walk and began to roost.

"Honk, honk!" said the gander, and he flew up into the tree.

"Honk, honk!" said the gray goose and she flew up into the tree.

"Honk, honk!" said all the other geese and they flew up into the tree.

When all the geese had roosted in the tree, the Little Old Woman said to herself:

"My rats and my geese have trimmed their tree very nicely. The rats with their red ribbons and their beads are as bright as little lights. The geese in their red coats are very handsome too.

"I was very clever to think of letting them trim their own tree. I am sure they enjoyed it. After all, half the fun of having a tree is in trimming it oneself.

"It was also a great help to me to be spared the trouble of making more trimming. Perhaps if I used my head I could think of other ways in which the geese and the rats could help me.

"But I will not use my head anymore now, for it is almost sundown. Then it will be Christmas Eve and I am planning to spend a quiet evening and enjoy myself."

19. How She Spent Christmas Eve

WHEN the sun went down and it was Christmas Eve the Little Old Woman went out and climbed up on the roof. She took a look at the star on the top of the Christmas tree. She looked at the stars in the sky too.

"The stars are large and clear and they shine very brightly tonight," she said.

"My star is shining brightly, too, and it is larger than any of them."

After a while she climbed down the ladder and came into the house.

She lit her lamp and set it on the table. Then she got ready to spend a quiet evening and enjoy herself. She sat down in her rocking-chair by the fire. She folded her arms across her apron and put her feet on her little footstool.

"What a lovely quiet Christmas Eve," she said to herself. "The geese and the rats are enjoying themselves in their tree and I am enjoying myself in my chair by the fire.

"I only hope that all the people in the whole world are as happy as we are.

"And what is more, they would be too, if they would do as I do and always use their heads."

Margaret Ruse